Mary's Tiger

Written by
Rex Harley

Illustrated by
Sue Porter

Gulliver Books

Harcourt Brace Jovanovich, Publishers

San Diego   New York   London

For two little tigers · Anne · Vaiha · Eve · Merina ·

HBJ

First published 1990 by Orchard Books
Text copyright © 1990 by Rex Harley
Illustration copyright © 1990 by Sue Porter

Requests for permission to make copies of any
part of the work should be mailed to:
Permissions Department,
Harcourt Brace Jovanovich, Publishers,
Orlando, Florida 32887.

Library of Congress Cataloging-in-Publication Data
Harley, Rex.
Mary's tiger/written by Rex Harley; illustrated by
Sue Porter.
p.   cm.
"Gulliver books."
Summary: The tiger in the picture Mary draws before
bedtime becomes a stuffed toy while she is asleep.
[1. Painting — Fiction. 2. Toys — Fiction. 3. Tigers —
Fiction.]
I. Porter, Sue. ill.. II. Title.
PZ7.H22657Mar   1990
[E] — dc20   89-49009

Printed in Belgium

First U.S. edition 1990
A B C D E

Mary loved to paint.

When Mrs. Morris said, "Why don't you fill up the whole page with a nice colorful picture?," Mary started to draw her favorite animal: a bright, stripy tiger.

She drew its head first. It was bigger than she'd planned.

So when she came to draw the tiger's body, it had to be very small, with little legs and a tiny tail.

Because it looked a bit unhappy scrunched up like that, Mary painted a huge smile on the tiger's face.

She showed the picture to her mother.

"What a lovely tiger," her mother said. "He looks very happy. Is he in love?"

Mary shook her head.

When Mary's father saw the picture he said, "What's he smiling for, Mary? Has he just had a tasty meal?"

"No," Mary said.

"What a funny-looking tiger," said her big brother, Paul. "Is he laughing at you?"

"No," said Mary. "You're all wrong." But she wouldn't tell them why he was smiling.

Mary's mother wanted to hang the painting on the kitchen wall with all Mary's other pictures.

But Mary wanted to put it in her bedroom.

She called the tiger Grin.
"Good night, Grin," she said at bedtime.
"Sleep well."

The room was very dark. Grin tried to sleep, but he could not get comfortable.

He wriggled and twisted around. He got himself into some very awkward positions.

And in the end he pushed so hard that he fell

off the paper and landed on the bed.

During the night Mary woke up to find her smiling tiger asleep on her pillow. He looked very comfortable.

Being careful not to wake him, she reached
up, took down the piece of blank paper, and
threw it away.

Then she climbed back into bed.

In the morning Mary's mother came to wake her. "Where's that lovely tiger of yours?" she asked.

"Don't worry," Mary said. "He's somewhere where he's happy." And they went down to breakfast.